READING CORNER

Hetty's New Hat

A humorous
farmyard story

First published in 2004 by
Franklin Watts
96 Leonard Street
London
EC2A 4XD

Franklin Watts Australia
45–51 Huntley Street
Alexandria
NSW 2015

Text © Margaret Nash 2004
Illustration © Martin Impey 2004

A CIP catalogue record for this book is available
from the British Library.

ISBN 0 7496 5308 6 (hbk)
ISBN 0 7496 5372 8 (pbk)

Series Editor: Jackie Hamley
Series Advisors: Dr Barrie Wade, Dr Hilary Minns
Design: Peter Scoulding

Printed in Hong Kong / China

READING CORNER

Hetty's New Hat

Written by
Margaret Nash

Illustrated by
Martin Impey

W
FRANKLIN WATTS
LONDON•SYDNEY

Margaret Nash

"I work in my study with the help of Tabitha, my cat, who sits on the chair beside me."

Martin Impey

"I work from a studio at the bottom of my garden, where I have lovely views of the countryside."

Hetty had a new hat.

"Oooh!" said the hens, "you DO look good in that hat!"

6

Hetty went for a walk
in her new hat.

Puff! Hetty's new hat
blew off her head!

11

The hat blew under the gate.

The hat blew across
the fields.

15

The hat blew past the
scarecrow ...

... and the horses.

The hat blew into the geese.

The hat blew over the pigs.

Then it landed.

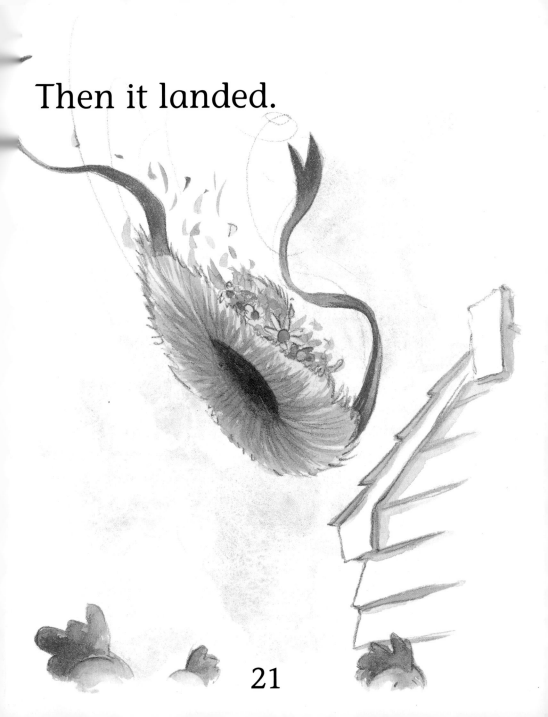

"Oooh!" said the hens, "you DO look good in that hat!"

Notes for parents and teachers

READING CORNER has been structured to provide maximum support for new readers. The stories may be used by adults for sharing with young children. Primarily, however, the stories are designed for newly independent readers, whether they are reading these books in bed at night, or in the reading corner at school or in the library.

Starting to read alone can be a daunting prospect. READING CORNER helps by providing visual support and repeating words and phrases, while making reading enjoyable. These books will develop confidence in the new reader, and encourage a love of reading that will last a lifetime!

If you are reading this book with a child, here are a few tips:

1. Make reading fun! Choose a time to read when you and the child are relaxed and have time to share the story.

2. Encourage children to reread the story, and to retell the story in their own words, using the illustrations to remind them what has happened.

3. Give praise! Remember that small mistakes need not always be corrected.

READING CORNER covers three grades of early reading ability, with three levels at each grade. Each level has a certain number of words per story, indicated by the number of bars on the spine of the book, to allow you to choose the right book for a young reader:

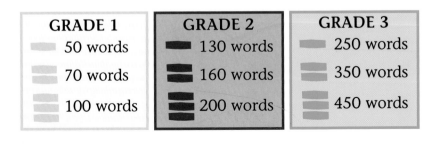

GRADE 1	GRADE 2	GRADE 3
50 words	130 words	250 words
70 words	160 words	350 words
100 words	200 words	450 words